The sea ponies swam up to the shallows and the girls climbed off their backs. The water was warm and beautifully clear. Little baby turtles swam by the shore and seahorses darted among patches of blue and purple seaweed…

Look out for more thrilling adventures!

The STORM DRAGON

The SKY UNICORN

The BABY FIREBIRD

The MAGIC FOX

The STAR WOLF

The Sea Pony

Paula Harrison

illustrated by SOPHY WILLIAMS

nosy crow

For Felicity Trew,
who loves sea ponies

First published in the UK in 2017 by Nosy Crow Ltd
The Crow's Nest, 10a Lant St
London, SE1 1QR, UK

A CIP catalogue record for this book will be available from the British Library

1 3 5 7 9 10 8 6 4 2

Printed and bound in the UK by Clays Ltd, St Ives Plc

Papers used by Nosy Crow are made from wood grown in sustainable forests.

ISBN: 978 0 85763 769 7

www.nosycrow.com

Chapter One
Surprise Visitors

Grace ran down the golden beach, her brown eyes sparkling with excitement. Sea ponies were leaping and galloping in the waves. Water drops glittered on their smooth white coats. Their brightly coloured tails and manes gleamed in the sunshine.

Grace stopped at the water's edge, feeling the warm sand under her feet and the waves lapping at her toes. A lighthouse with white and orange stripes towered on the clifftop behind her. Palm trees swayed gently in the breeze. Further along

the bay was a cluster of colourful houses. This was Cala Sands, the village where Grace lived.

Every day Grace's cousins sailed out of the harbour on their fishing boat. Grace went with them to catch fish to sell at the market. She loved sailing, but she loved coming to the beach to see the ponies even more!

The ponies jumped high, splashing each other with their hooves. They were beautiful creatures with bright patterns across their manes and tails. Grace's favourite sea pony had a rainbow pattern that gleamed every time she sprang into the air. She looked a little younger than the other ponies and she was full of energy. All the sea ponies could jump, but this pony sprang higher than all the others!

Kicking off her sandals, Grace ran into the shallows and waded out to where the water got deeper. The sea ponies neighed happily when they saw her. The one with the rainbow tail flicked water into the air with her nose,

as if she wanted Grace to come and play.

Grace grinned and splashed water back with her hands. Being friends with the sea ponies was the best thing about living in Cala Sands.

There were lots of magical creatures in the Kingdom of Arramia – sky unicorns, dragons and firebirds – but she was sure none of them were as wonderful as the sea ponies! They had the power to bring peace to the waves by using special movements that looked almost like a dance. Grace had seen them calm the stormy sea many times to help the fishing boats.

She dived under the surface without worrying about her wet shorts and top. The water was warm and everything would dry quickly in the sun afterwards. Little silver fish darted through the turquoise water. Pink shells gleamed among the pebbles on the ocean floor.

The waves rocked Grace gently as she bobbed back to the surface.

The rainbow sea pony flicked her tail and dived under the water before popping up a little further away. Grace laughed and tried to catch up with her. Grace was a strong swimmer but she knew she could never be as good as the sea

ponies! They moved so gracefully through the water. The rainbow pony jumped high and soon all the sea ponies were leaping and splashing too.

Suddenly a shadow fell across the water and blocked out the sunshine. The sea ponies neighed as if they were talking to each other. Then they dived under the waves and swam out to sea.

"Don't go!" called Grace, but the sea ponies were already far away.

Swimming back to the beach, she climbed on to the sand and squeezed the water out of her curly black hair. She glanced at the sky, expecting to see a raincloud blocking out the sun. Instead she saw a creature zooming towards the beach.

As it got closer, Grace saw that it was actually two creatures. From a distance, the smaller one looked like a white horse. Its hooves left a sparkling trail in the air. The bigger one was a dragon with huge leathery wings.

Grace's heart raced. She was used to seeing sea dragons – they were small blue creatures that lived on the Island of Ixus out in the bay. The island was said to be an amazing place where no humans lived at all. Grace desperately wanted to go there someday. But this dragon in the sky wasn't a little sea dragon. This was a full-size storm dragon and it was flying right next to a sky unicorn!

The dragon and the unicorn swooped low over the water and landed on the sand not far

from Grace.

A girl with blonde hair jumped down from the dragon's back, rushed into the waves and joyfully flicked water into the air. "Maya! Windrunner!" she called back. "I'm standing in the Great Ocean. I can't believe it! I've never even *seen* the ocean before!"

"Sophy, come back!" A girl with smooth dark hair climbed down from the sky unicorn's back, laughing at her friend. "There's someone else here – look!" She came towards Grace, smiling. "Hello, I'm Maya. I hope we didn't startle you. We needed somewhere to land for a rest. We've been flying for ages."

Grace stared at her, a thousand questions whizzing around her head. "Hello, I'm Grace. Where are you from? I've never seen anyone flying on a dragon or a sky unicorn before."

"We've come from the Emerald Plain,"

said Maya, smiling. "We started off in a town called Blyford next to Misty Lake. My family and I had sailed there on our boats because we're travelling performers. That's where I met Sophy."

"That's me! I'm Sophy from Greytowers Castle." The blonde-haired girl bounced up to them. "Is this Cala Sands Bay? And have you seen any sea ponies lately?"

"Yes, this is Cala Sands Bay." Grace frowned. Why was this girl asking about the ponies? "There were some sea ponies here a minute ago but they swam away. Did you come here to meet them?"

Sophy leaned over to whisper something in Maya's ear. The other girl shook her head and murmured something back.

Grace folded her arms. She didn't like people keeping secrets from her. It happened to her all the time with her cousins, who thought she was still a baby even though she could hoist a sail

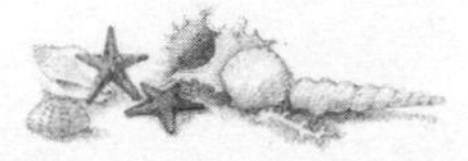

and cast a fishing net just as well as them!

She was about to turn away when she felt a nudge at her elbow. The sky unicorn was standing by her side, the golden horn on its forehead gleaming in the sun. Its coat and mane were snowy white, and its tail was a beautiful pale green.

"Hello, girl!" said Grace, softly stroking her nose. "What's your name?"

"She's called Marella," Maya told her. "And the storm dragon's name is Windrunner."

The dragon bowed his head in greeting. A little gust of wind swirled across the beach.

"Do you like magical animals, Grace?" asked Sophy, her brow creasing. "Do you think people should be kind to them?"

"Of course I do!" said Grace. "They're so special! Although I think we should be kind to *all* animals."

"I told you!" Maya said to Sophy. "We should tell her. She might be able to help us."

"Help you with what?" Grace felt that if they didn't tell her their secret soon, she'd burst!

"We've come here to help magical animals in danger," Sophy told her. "You see, I'm a maid at Greytowers Castle where the queen lives. There's a wicked knight called Sir Fitzroy living there too and he's persuaded the queen that all magical creatures should be captured. He's sent letters to his supporters all over the kingdom ordering them to catch every magical animal they can find."

"That's horrible!" cried Grace. "How could he do that?"

Sophy shook her head. "He's a bad man. He hates the magical animals and he's telling everyone they're too dangerous to be free."

"We rescued a unicorn foal together at Misty Lake," added Maya. "Sir Fitzroy was really cross about that!"

"After that we went on different adventures and helped to rescue other magical creatures

like firebirds and star wolves," said Sophy. "But when I heard that the sea ponies could be in danger I knew I had to fetch Maya and come right away!"

The unicorn brushed against Maya's shoulder and made a long whinnying sound.

"That's right, Marella. I'd forgotten!" said Maya. "There's meant to be a large boat that's hunting for the sea ponies—"

"Wait a minute!" interrupted Grace. "Did you just talk to the unicorn?"

Maya blushed. "Yes I did!"

"We can both talk to

magical animals," said Sophy proudly.

"But how?" gasped Grace.

Sophy pulled a thread from around her neck. Hanging on the end of the necklace was a rough grey stone. "I can show you if you like, but you have to promise not to tell anyone!"

She unwound the thread from the stone and pulled it gently, so that it opened into two pieces. Inside each part was a hollow filled with gleaming purple crystals. "This is how I speak to magical creatures. There's magic in this stone that lets me talk to them whenever I like!"

Chapter Two
The Royal Stickleback

Grace gazed at Sophy's magic stone. "That's amazing! Where did you get it from? And how did you know it was magical?"

"It all happened by accident," Sophy told her. "The queen was throwing out some old belongings and there it was among the things she cast away."

"I have one too!" Maya pulled out her own stone, which was filled with emerald-green crystals. "The magic inside each Speaking Stone only works for one person. So we can't

use each other's."

"I've met new friends – Talia, Lucas and Emma – and they all found a stone that worked," added Sophy. "And maybe, if we're lucky, there will be one for you too!" She reached into her pocket and took out a little bag made from purple velvet.

"Really? Then I'd be able to talk to magical animals as well?" Grace longed to speak to the sea pony with the rainbow tail. They'd played together so many times. Talking to her would be the best thing ever!

"Yes, you would! Now, let's see…" Sophy knelt down on the beach and emptied a handful of rocks on to the sand. "Touch this one. See if that works." She handed Grace one of the stones.

Grace turned it over, running her fingers over its rough grey edges. But it didn't open into two pieces with a tiny hidden cave inside like the other girls' stones. It sat in her hand – nothing

more than a dull grey rock. "Am I supposed to do something? I don't know if I'm doing this right."

"Try touching a different stone!" said Maya eagerly. "We don't know which one is supposed to be yours."

Grace picked up the stones one by one, excitement fizzing inside her. She held each one for a moment before putting it down and trying another. "Is this right? Is something meant to happen?"

"First the stone will get hot and then it'll break open all by itself," Sophy told her. "Try another one!"

Grace picked up another and another. Finally she touched the last one. None of the stones had changed at all.

Grace swallowed, trying not to show her disappointment. "Maybe there isn't a magical stone for me after all."

"I'm really sorry, Grace." Maya bit her lip.

"You like animals so much that I was sure there'd be one for you."

"You will still help us, won't you?" said Sophy as she gathered the stones into the little bag again. "We've never been here before and you must know where to find everything."

"Of course I'll help!" A determined look grew in Grace's eyes. "I love the sea ponies and I wouldn't let anyone hurt them!"

Sophy and Maya said goodbye to their dragon and unicorn friends, who wanted to fly home to their families. Windrunner, the storm dragon, promised to return when the girls needed him again.

Grace led the girls up the cliff path, past the lighthouse and across the field towards Cala Sands. "I sometimes spot the sea ponies when I'm out fishing with my cousins," she told them. "Maybe you could come with us tomorrow."

"Do you know anyone who might want to harm the ponies?" asked Maya.

Grace frowned. "Lady Cavendish doesn't like animals much but she never goes out on her boat. Here we are!" She pointed to the cluster of houses at the bottom of the hill.

Cala Sands had a pretty harbour full of fishing boats. Little cottages in blue, yellow and pink crowded round the waterfront. A nearby bakery had opened its doors and the delicious smcll of brcad and cakes drifted down the street.

"Which is your boat, Grace?" asked Maya.

"That one!" Grace pointed to a neat purple boat with a brightly polished nameplate. "It's called *The Leaping Sea Pony*. It's not really mine. It belongs to my cousins."

"What a lovely boat! It's much nicer than that big ship over there." Sophy glanced at a larger boat with several men on the deck. "*The Royal Stickleback* – what an awful name!"

"I know!" agreed Grace. "Sticklebacks don't even live in the sea. They're fish that live in rivers, so it's a silly name for an ocean boat."

As she spoke, a woman dressed in rich clothes came out on to the deck of *The Royal Stickleback* and began giving orders to the men. Her dark hair was combed back from her face and she wore a long elegant dress that looked strange next to the men's muddy boots and overalls.

"That's Lady Cavendish," hissed Grace. "She owns the harbour, so we're all supposed to be nice to her. Her ship is the biggest in Cala Sands

but I've never seen her go on board before."

"Maybe we should find out what's she up to," said Sophy.

The three girls crept along by the harbour wall until they were close enough to hear. Lady Cavendish was telling the men to prepare to set sail. The sailors rolled up a huge net and stowed it next to the cabin. Then one man climbed the rigging and pulled out a long telescope.

"Find me the sea ponies," Lady Cavendish called up to him. "I have received a message from Sir Fitzroy – the queen's chief knight. All magical sea creatures must be captured. They are a danger to us all!"

"There's no sign of any sea ponies, My Lady," the sailor called down. "No, wait! There's a herd of them just there, across the bay."

"Set sail!" screeched Lady Cavendish. "We must catch the little beasts!"

Sophy turned to the others, her face pale. "She's after the sea ponies! What shall we do?"

Grace's brown eyes turned fierce. "I know! We can block her ship." She pelted back to *The Leaping Sea Pony* and untied the mooring rope. "Sophy! Maya! Come and help me with the oars."

Sophy and Maya scrambled on to the boat. Grace threw the mooring rope on to the deck and leapt after it. Then she and Maya each took a pair of oars and rowed across the harbour while Sophy acted as lookout.

"*The Royal Stickleback*'s heading for the harbour entrance," said Sophy.

"We can still beat them," panted Grace. "Their ship is much bigger and heavier. It will

move slower than ours."

Lady Cavendish's voice could be heard across the water, shrieking at the men to make the ship go faster.

Rowing hard, the girls brought *The Leaping Sea Pony* to the mouth of the harbour where the gap in the wall led out to the open sea.

"Quick, Sophy!" hissed Grace. "Drop the anchor."

Sophy dropped the heavy anchor overboard and the boat came to a stop. *The Royal Stickleback* had to turn sideways to avoid bumping into them.

"What are you doing, girl?" shouted Lady Cavendish. "You're blocking the way. Move aside at once!"

"Just a second, My Lady. The sail won't work until I do this knot. I must tie it right away." Grace knelt down and began tying a knot in the sail rope really slowly.

Lady Cavendish tapped her foot against the deck, her face turning red. "Girl! I said move *immediately*!"

Grace finished her knot and stood up. "Are you in a hurry, Lady Cavendish? I hope nothing's wrong."

The crew of *The Royal Stickleback* exchanged surprised looks. No one usually questioned Lady Cavendish.

"Of course I'm in a hurry, stupid girl!" said her ladyship. "Yesterday I received a message from the most important knight in the land, Sir Fitzroy, giving instructions to capture the beasts ruining our ocean. Then, just as we spy the

creatures coming across the bay, you get in the way and spoil it all!"

"But, Lady Cavendish!" Grace burst out. "If you're talking about the sea ponies, they never ruin anything. Sometimes their special movements calm the waves and that makes it easier for us all to catch our fish. It's magic!"

"No animal should be allowed to have magic," snapped Lady Cavendish. "They're nothing but sly little beasts and they won't be so magical once they're trapped in the extra-large net I've brought."

"The sea ponies have gone now, My Lady," called the man in the rigging. "We'd do better to follow them tomorrow when the tide is in our favour."

"Very well!" Lady Cavendish clicked her fingers. "Take us back to the jetty for now. Tomorrow we'll hunt them all down. One by one."

Chapter Three
Mr Wetherstone's Lighthouse

Grace, Maya and Sophy rowed their boat back to its mooring place and climbed ashore. Lady Cavendish was still shouting orders at her crew as the girls left the harbour.

"The trouble is, we've only stopped her for now," said Sophy gloomily. "Tomorrow she'll set sail and hunt for the sea ponies again."

"That gives us the rest of the day to make a plan." Grace led them into the bakery. "Come on, we won't get any good ideas on an empty stomach."

The girls bought bread rolls, some purple moonfruit and a delicious-looking cherry cake. Then Grace took them out of the village towards the clifftop. "I want to show you the lighthouse. You can see the whole of Cala Sands Bay from the top. Mr Wetherstone is the lighthouse keeper and he likes to have visitors. Sometimes he makes me a chocolate milkshake."

"Oh, I hope he'll make us some too!" said Sophy. "I'm really thirsty."

The stripy lighthouse stood on the cliff behind the beach. The tall tower had a circular window all the way round the top for the light to shine through at night.

Grace knocked on the door. It was opened by a man with grey hair and twinkly brown eyes.

"Afternoon, Grace," he said. "I see you've brought some friends with you today."

"Hello, Mr Wetherstone! This is Sophy and Maya," said Grace. "Can we come in?"

"Of course!" The old man smiled and led them into the cosy round room. "Welcome to my lighthouse. Come in and make yourselves at home."

Large red armchairs stood against the curved walls, which were covered with old maps and paintings of the sea. A spiral staircase in the corner wound all the way to the top of the tower.

Grace cut the cherry cake into slices and handed them to everyone. Mr Wetherstone made four glasses of chocolate milkshake in the kitchen upstairs.

"Thank you, Mr Wetherstone," said Grace, sipping from her glass.

The lighthouse keeper smiled. "Any good news from the harbour, Grace? Has the fishing gone well?"

"There's bad news!" Grace's face clouded over. She told Mr Wetherstone about Lady Cavendish and the sea ponies. Sophy and Maya

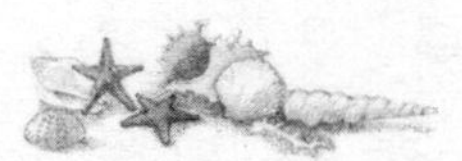

added some details too.

Mr Wetherstone listened and nodded wisely. "So Lady Cavendish is obeying the orders of this knight, Sir Fitzroy, to hunt the magical animals," he said as Grace finished. "I'm afraid I'm not surprised."

"But why doesn't she realise that the sea ponies are amazing?" Grace burst out. "Why can't she see they should be protected?"

"People don't understand magic, and some people are afraid of things they don't understand," said Mr Wetherstone.

"Maybe there's a way we can change her mind about the sea ponies," said Maya hopefully.

Grace shook her head. "I don't think that will work. She thinks she rules Cala Sands and she never listens to anyone! We have to find a way to stop her. I just don't know how."

"You're kind, clever girls. I believe you'll find a way." Mr Wetherstone rose from his seat. "Now,

I must buy some oil to keep the lamp in the lighthouse burning tonight. Stay here as long as you like."

"Thank you!" said Maya and Sophy.

"Thanks, Mr Wetherstone. See you soon!" added Grace.

After the girls finished their cake, they climbed to the top of the lighthouse where the curved window gave them a perfect view of the ocean.

"See that silvery line far out to sea?" Grace pointed into the distance. "That's the Island of Ixus where the sea dragons live. It's said to be a really magical place. I want to go there one day when I have my own boat. My cousins won't let me take the fishing boat because they think it's too far."

"It sounds brilliant!" said Maya.

"The whole ocean is amazing!" said Sophy, leaning close to the window. "Lady Cavendish is so silly wanting to spoil things by hurting the sea ponies."

Maya gave a little shiver. "I wonder how she got the idea for using an extra-large net to catch the poor creatures. Do you think she got her crew to join lots of smaller nets together?"

"Maybe..." Grace stared at the white-flecked waves that danced on the ocean.

"What is it, Grace?" asked Sophy.

Grace rubbed her ear. "It's that net. I'm just thinking..." She stared out of the window and frowned for a minute before turning to the others. "That's it! I know how we can ruin all of Lady Cavendish's plans!"

"How?" said Maya and Sophy eagerly.

"All we need to do is cut that big net," Grace told them. "We can chop it so the holes are big enough for the sea ponies to swim through. Lady Cavendish will never realise until it's too late!"

The girls grinned at each other.

"I think that would work really well!" said Sophy.

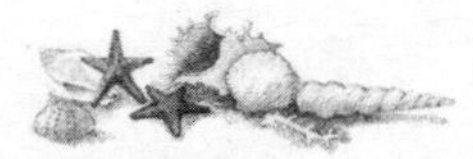

"It's a great idea," agreed Maya. "We just need to wait till her crew have gone home before we sneak on to her boat. We don't want anyone to see us."

Grace, Maya and Sophy waited until the sun sank low over the Great Ocean, casting golden light across the rippling water. As daylight faded, they took the path to the village and crept down to the harbour.

The waterfront was empty. The only sound was the creaking of the wooden boats and the slapping of water against the harbour wall.

Grace climbed aboard her cousins' boat, *The Leaping Sea Pony*, and rummaged quickly through the tools her cousins kept in a small box. Luckily there was a large pair of scissors. She just hoped they would be strong enough to cut the net.

Sneaking along the harbour, they climbed on to *The Royal Stickleback*.

"Here it is!" Sophy took hold of the rolled-up net. "I'll take this end and you two take the other end."

Carefully, they unwound the extra-large net, which stretched almost across the whole deck.

"Look at the size of it!" groaned Grace. "It's going to take us a long time to cut all the holes."

"Shh!" Maya laid a warning hand on her arm.

Two figures with a lamp came down the street that led to the waterfront. The girls froze but the people walked on without turning into the harbour.

"It's all right, they've gone," said Sophy. "Shall

we take turns with the scissors then?"

"Sure! Why don't I go first?" Grace got the scissors into position and tried to squeeze them shut. She had to use both hands. It took a few goes before she managed to close them over the tough netting.

Sophy and Maya pulled the net straight to make it easier. Grace dug the scissors in again and kept cutting. Soon there was a square of snipped net large enough for a sea pony to swim through.

"Do you really think this will work?" whispered Maya.

Grace smiled and handed her the scissors. "It has to! Here you are! You can have the next turn."

As she held the net still for Maya, Grace thought of the playful sea horse with the rainbow-coloured mane and tail. She would never let anyone hurt that lovely pony.

Chapter Four
Stowaways

The three girls carried on snipping the net as the sky grew darker and darker. A bright full moon rose, casting a pale shimmering reflection on the water. The moonlight made it easier to see. Passing the scissors between them, the girls kept on cutting the net and making the holes wider.

By the time they had each taken four turns their legs ached from sitting on the hard wooden deck. Grace rubbed her hands together. They felt sore from working the scissors.

"I wonder what time it is," said Sophy with a yawn. "We must have been working for hours."

"Do you think we've cut enough holes yet?" Grace gazed at the net. Large rips were spread all the way across it. Little bits of loose netting were scattered over the deck.

"I think we've done a lot." Maya picked up some scraps of net. "We'd better tidy up these loose bits. If Lady Cavendish sees them she might guess what we've done."

The girls gathered the little bits of net and hid them in an empty bucket by the rigging.

"That was hard work!" Sophy rubbed her eyes. "I'm really hungry."

"I still have the rest of the cherry cake," said Grace, producing the parcel of wrapped-up cake from her pocket.

"Let's eat it in the cabin," suggested Maya. "It's getting cold out here."

They rolled the net to one side. Grace picked up the scissors to make sure they didn't lose them. Then they climbed down the steps into the cabin.

Grace stared round in amazement. Velvet curtains lined the cabin windows. In the middle was a table covered with a snow-white cloth, and set with golden plates and crystal glasses. "Wow! It's like a cabin for a queen."

"Maybe Lady Cavendish thinks she *should* be the queen," giggled Sophy.

"Making a cabin look fancy is just silly!" said Grace. "Sailing a boat is about feeling the rise and fall of the waves. It's about watching the seagulls swooping. It's about looking for turtles and sea ponies, not sitting down here eating food off golden plates!"

"Did you hear something?" said Maya.

"It was probably my stomach rumbling," Sophy told her. "Hurry up and share the cake out, Grace."

Grace took no notice. Her eyes shone as she thought of all the things she loved about the sea. "You see … sailing is all about sniffing the salty air and seeing miles and miles of ocean all around you—"

Maya twisted round, her face anxious. "I really think I heard something!"

"It's about watching fish dart between the rocks and feeling the sea breeze on your face and—"

"Sshh, Grace!" said Maya, right into her ear.

"I think someone's coming!"

Sophy bounded to the door of the cabin. "There are people on the deck," she hissed. "I can't see how many..."

"What are they doing here in the middle of the night?" said Grace, snapping out of her daydream. "They can't have heard us. We were so quiet."

Maya pointed to the pale light seeping through the window. "It's not the middle of the night any more – look!"

"You're right. We must have been here the whole night!" Grace peeked round the cabin door. "If Lady Cavendish and her crew have decided to set sail early, there's no way we'll get out of here without being seen."

"Maybe we can sneak past them," said Sophy.

Heavy footsteps thumped overhead and the girls shrank back from the door.

"We can't!" whispered Grace. "They'll spot us for sure and all the work we did on the net will

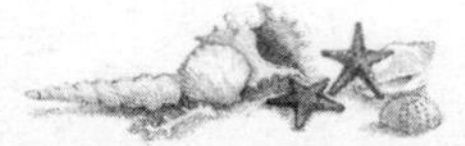

be for nothing. We have to hide!"

Lady Cavendish's voice drifted into the cabin and the girls looked around in panic. Grace saw a gap between a cupboard and the wall that was big enough to hide in. "Maya, in here!" She pulled Maya into the space and squeezed in next to her, while Sophy hid behind the curtain.

The clacking of high-heeled shoes sounded on the steps. "I want things done properly," said Lady Cavendish. "Everything should be absolutely neat and tidy. Someone left that net half unrolled. There's no excuse for it!"

The cabin door creaked open and Lady Cavendish swished inside wearing a long black cloak. Bracelets jangled on her wrists.

"I assure you, My Lady, everything will be done properly," a man called down from the deck. "We'll catch these beasts before the day is over. Then we'll take them to the market in that wooden tank just as you planned."

"Yes, yes! Off you go and get started," replied Lady Cavendish.

Grace could hardly breathe. They were going to put the sea ponies in a tank! What a horrible idea. The poor things would be crammed in with no room to move. And after being sold at the market they could end up anywhere! This was even worse than she'd thought.

Leaning out a bit, Grace managed to see round the side of the cupboard. Lady Cavendish had sat down and placed a small telescope on the table. She took off her velvet cloak. Then she opened a basket by her feet and picked out some crackers, which she began to spread with a strange green paste. Grace thought it looked a bit like mushed-up seaweed.

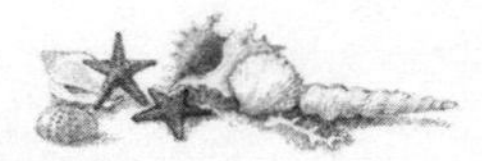

Lady Cavendish ate the crackers one after the other, very slowly. Grace started to fidget. How long would they have to stay squeezed into this gap, hardly able to breathe? Maya nudged her but Grace couldn't stop wriggling. She desperately wanted to scratch her head but there was no room to stretch out and do it.

At last Lady Cavendish stopped eating and left the cabin. The girls tumbled out of their hiding places.

"I thought she'd never go!" gasped Maya.

"Are you sure we shouldn't try to sneak off the boat?" asked Sophy. "Hiding is going to be pretty tricky, especially if she keeps coming down here for a picnic!"

There was a shout from the deck above, followed by a bumping noise. The ship rocked as it moved across the harbour.

"It's too late!" Grace's eyes gleamed. "Now we're stowaways! We may as well have some fun." She picked up Lady Cavendish's telescope.

"They won't be able to spot the sea ponies so easily without this. Where shall we hide it?"

Maya's mouth dropped open. "Grace, how do you *dare*?"

"Well, she's planning to capture the sea ponies so we should do everything we can to stop her, even if it *is* a bit sneaky!" said Grace firmly.

"I guess you're right," said Maya. "So where shall we put it?"

"Here!" Sophy pulled open the cupboard, which was full of more golden plates and lacy napkins.

Grace shoved the telescope right at the back behind a stack of silver knives and forks. Then she turned back to the table. "What other pranks can we play? Let's make Lady Cavendish as muddled as possible. Then she won't have time to hunt for the sea ponies!"

Chapter Five
Tricks and Mischief

Grace, Maya and Sophy stared round the cabin, wondering what other tricks they could play on Lady Cavendish to delay her hunt for the sea ponies!

"We could hide her crackers," suggested Maya.

"We could tie her cloak to the sail rope," said Sophy.

The girls went round the cabin, messing everything up. Even the green paste, which Lady Cavendish had spread on her crackers, was naughtily smeared on to the golden plates to give them a strange mouldy look.

Giggling, the girls sneaked up the cabin steps and hid behind some wooden crates that were piled up on the deck. A moment later Lady Cavendish went down to the cabin and gave a terrible shriek.

"Who's made all this mess?" She climbed back to the deck and glared at the crew. "It looks as if an animal has been in the cabin. Someone even stole my crackers! Which of you did this?"

The men shook their heads.

"I'm sure no one went down there, My Lady," said a sailor with a beard.

Grace, Maya and Sophy stayed hidden behind the wooden crates.

"Someone must know what happened." Lady Cavendish scowled at her crew. "Get down there and clear it up straight away."

Some of the sailors trooped into the cabin to follow her order. After a lot of banging, clanking

and complaining, they climbed out again.

"It's done, My Lady," said the sailor with the beard. "May I take the telescope now? It'll help me spot the sea ponies."

Lady Cavendish disappeared into the cabin, muttering to herself. "I don't believe it!" she cried. "I left the telescope here on the table. Who's stolen it?"

Two of the men followed her into the cabin to help her look but they all came out empty handed. The bearded man climbed the rigging without the telescope and Lady Cavendish marched crossly up and down the deck.

Grace, Maya and Sophy began to feel cold crouching behind the wooden boxes. The sun rose in the sky and the harbour shrank in the distance.

"We're a long way from land," whispered Sophy. "Do you think they'll find the sea ponies without a telescope, Grace?"

"I don't know," replied Grace. "I wish there

was a way to warn the ponies not to come near this boat."

As the morning went on, the girls began to hope that the crew were searching in the wrong place. The wind and waves grew stronger. Lady Cavendish stood at the stern of the ship, glaring out to sea.

"Sea ponies ahoy!" shouted the man in the rigging. "There are twelve of them on the starboard side."

Lady Cavendish rushed to the right hand side of the ship, eagerly scanning the waves. Grace peered over the top of the crates and her heart sank. A dozen sea ponies with gleaming white coats came leaping and galloping through the water. When they saw the ship they swam towards it, neighing to each other.

"Get ready with the net!" shouted Lady Cavendish.

Three of the crew hoisted the net between them. The sea ponies swam closer, their bright

tails swishing through the water. Two of the creatures sprang into the air, the water glittering on their tails.

"Now!" screamed Lady Cavendish.

The men threw the net out into the ocean. It fell across a large stretch of water, trapping four sea ponies. The animals struggled underneath the mesh. One of them had a rainbow pattern on its mane and tail.

"No! You can't do that!" Grace cried, dashing out from behind the boxes.

"Grace!" hissed Sophy. "Wait and see if our plan works."

Grace took no notice. She leaned over the side of the boat, staring at her beloved rainbow pony. Twisting and turning, the four captured animals kicked the net with their hooves. The free sea ponies circled around the trapped ones, calling anxiously.

Lady Cavendish was glaring at the trapped sea ponies and didn't notice Grace, who was

hidden by the sail. "What are you waiting for?" she called to the men. "Pull the net back in!"

Maya and Sophy crept out of hiding and joined Grace.

"Maybe we didn't make the holes large enough." Grace twisted her hands together. "Maybe the sea ponies can't find them."

"Sea ponies!" Sophy called to the magical creatures. "There are big holes in the net that you can swim through."

The sea ponies looked up in surprise as they understood Sophy's words. There was a shout from behind as some of the crew spotted the girls. Sophy, Maya and Grace took no notice of the sailors.

"All you have to do is find one of the big holes," called Maya. "Then just dive through."

Grace clasped her hands together tightly. She wished she could call to the sea ponies too but she didn't have a special stone that let her talk to magical animals. They wouldn't understand her at all. A lump came to her throat as she watched the trapped creatures struggling under the net. "Please, *please* find the holes we made," she whispered. "You can do it! I believe in you."

The free sea ponies called to the trapped ones. Their neighs and whinnies grew more and more urgent.

"It's all right!" Maya's eyes sparkled. "They've spotted the holes in the net."

The men began to draw the net tighter. The four trapped sea ponies wriggled and squirmed, looking for the holes where the girls had cut the mesh. The free sea ponies circled round them,

calling out encouragement.

One captured pony struggled free and swam to join the others. The magical creature jumped with happiness at its escape and flicked water high in the air with its nose.

"It's working!" Grace grinned widely. "It's really working!"

"Fools, what have you done!" cried Lady Cavendish. "The beasts are escaping!"

The men hauled the net in faster.

Two more sea ponies broke free from the net.

"That's brilliant!" Sophy called to the sea ponies.

"I knew you could do it," said Maya.

Hearing the girls' voices, Lady Cavendish peered round the main sail. "What's going on? What are *you* doing here? Never mind! I'll deal with you in a minute." She marched up the deck, shouting at the men to pull the net in faster.

There was a frantic neighing from below. One sea pony was still trapped inside the net. It was Grace's favourite – the pony with the rainbow-coloured mane and tail.

Grace's stomach lurched. What if she couldn't get free? For a terrible moment, she thought the

poor thing would be dragged out of the water, but at the last second the rainbow pony dived through a gap in the mesh. The men pulled in the rest of the net, catching nothing but seaweed.

"She's free!" Grace jumped up and down as the sea pony swam to join her friends.

"You pest of a girl!" Lady Cavendish reached Grace's side in an instant. "There is nothing to celebrate. These dreadful animals need to be caught and contained. Now, tell me what you're doing here AT ONCE!"

Grace's mind went blank. She couldn't think of a single thing to say.

"We … um … came to look for something," began Maya.

"But we didn't mean to stow away," said Sophy. "It was an accident really."

"An accident!" Lady Cavendish fixed her cold grey eyes on them. "I don't believe anything you girls do is an accident. There's something very suspicious about all of this."

Before she could question them further, the men with the net interrupted her. "Do you want us to give chase, My Lady? The creatures are heading towards Lighthouse Rocks but I think we might be able to catch them."

"Of course I want you to give chase!" snapped Lady Cavendish. "What are you waiting for?"

The men hurried away to hoist more sails. Lady Cavendish picked up a bucket, a bar of soap and a bundle of old rags, and threw them at the girls.

"There you are!" she snapped. "Make yourselves useful. Fill that bucket with water and start scrubbing the deck right now, otherwise I'll have you all thrown overboard."

Maya nudged Grace, who was scowling, and they all got down on their knees and scrubbed the deck with the rags.

"I don't care though!" whispered Sophy. "I'll scrub the deck all day as long as the sea ponies are free."

"I just hope they don't work out what happened to the net," said Maya, glancing nervously at Lady Cavendish.

"Our plan worked!" Grace smiled. "That's all that matters."

Chapter Six
Danger at Lighthouse Rocks

Some of the men studied the broken net. One of them found the large holes and began looking suspiciously at the girls.

"Stop wasting time and start searching for the sea ponies!" Lady Cavendish told the men. "We MUST catch them before they get too far away."

The men hoisted another sail and the ship leapt forwards. The wind grew stronger, making the sails billow and the mast creak. The twelve sea ponies were spotted not far away, galloping

through the water.

Grace scrubbed the deck, wishing there was a way to persuade Lady Cavendish to turn the ship round. All the sea ponies had escaped, but what if the men hauled the net in faster next time?

"Get that one!" ordered Lady Cavendish. "It's slower than the rest."

Grace's heart sank and she scrambled up to see what was happening. The rainbow pony had fallen behind the rest of the herd. Her hooves dragged in the water and her tail was hardly moving.

"What is it, Grace?" whispered Maya.

Grace dashed to the side of the ship, followed by Maya and Sophy. "It's the rainbow pony. Look, she's hurt."

A chunk of net was wedged over the pony's legs, making it impossible for her to gallop properly. Without using her hooves, she couldn't leap or dive. She struggled through the water, her tail dragging behind her.

"Maya! Sophy!" hissed Grace. "I need you to distract everyone while I get into the water and help the pony. Can you do that?"

Sophy nodded quickly. "We'll think of something!"

"Good luck!" said Maya.

Grace darted across the deck, hiding behind the wooden crates as one of the crew passed by. She wanted to reach the far corner where she could slip into the sea without anyone noticing.

Maya and Sophy ran to find the scissors they'd used on the net. Working quickly, they hacked at the thick rope that held up the smaller sail. The rope broke and one end of the sail flapped wildly in the wind. The boat slowed down.

Sophy hid the scissors and both girls pretended they were still scrubbing the deck. Lady Cavendish began shouting orders and the crew ran up and down the boat, trying to grab the loose sail.

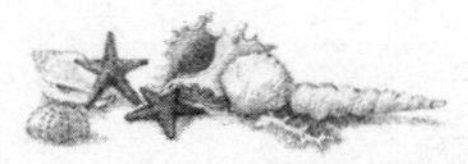

Grace's heart beat faster as she climbed on to the edge of the boat. She had to do this now while no one was looking.

Springing into the air, she dived gracefully into the turquoise ocean. The warm water closed around her. Shoals of pink and orange fish darted out of her way. Grace swam by a golden starfish, past clumps of pale-green seaweed that swayed with the water's current.

Rays of sunlight broke through the surface and danced on the sandy seabed far below.

Grace pulled upwards and swam quickly to the injured sea pony. The creature snorted and nodded her head weakly to show she was glad to see Grace.

"You poor thing!" said Grace. "It must be awful trying to swim with this net stuck to you." Gently, she checked the pony's leg and found the piece of net twisted tightly around her skin. The sea pony gave a high whinny, as if it was sore.

"Don't worry, I'll be careful." Treading water to keep afloat, Grace struggled with the tangled mesh. "I wish I knew your name," she sighed. "I suppose if one of the magical stones had worked, I'd be able to ask you."

The pony looked at her with bright eyes and gave another whinny.

"There!" Grace pulled the last bit of the net away. "Now you can swim properly again!"

The sea pony whickered in delight and shook

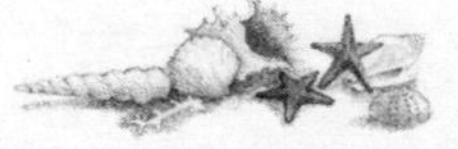

her mane.

"That's OK!" Grace laughed. "I know you'd help me if I was in trouble."

She turned to see what had happened to the ship and gasped. While she had been untangling the rainbow pony, the creature's friends had returned to look for her. Lady Cavendish, excited at the sight of so many sea ponies, was ordering the crew to steer towards them.

Grace knew the ship was in real danger.

Hidden just beneath the water was a circle of dangerously sharp rocks. The only sign of where the rocks lay were patches of white surf on the waves above. They were called Lighthouse Rocks because the lighthouse on the clifftop had been placed there to warn boats away from them.

Grace had sailed past here many times in her fishing boat. Her cousins had always warned her to be careful. The rocks could be deadly.

"Hey!" Grace waved her arms, trying to get the attention of Lady Cavendish and the crew. "Stop! You're right next to Lighthouse Rocks!"

Lady Cavendish and the crew were too busy with the sea ponies to notice her.

"Hey!" Grace tried again. "You're too close to the rocks. You're going to crash!"

Lady Cavendish had taken control of the ship's wheel, turning it towards the rocks. Her eyes glinted greedily.

Boom! A terrible crash was followed by an

awful scraping noise. The ship shuddered and the crew ran to the side to see what was wrong.

"Abandon ship!" shrieked Lady Cavendish.

Her crew ignored her order. Instead they hoisted a larger sail to change the ship's direction.

"What are you doing, you fools!" cried Lady Cavendish. "It's useless! The sea ponies lured us on to these rocks. That was their plan all along!"

The ship trembled as its wooden sides scraped against the rocks.

Treading water, Grace thought quickly. Sophy and Maya were on that boat. There had to be a way to get help. "Sophy! Maya!" she shouted. "Where is your friend, the dragon?"

The other girls waved back to show they'd heard and understood. Above the noise of the waves, Grace heard them whistle a strange high-pitched melody and she saw a little golden songbird swoop down to the boat.

Grace watched anxiously. How long would

it take for Sophy and Maya's dragon to get here? Were her new friends in terrible danger? The waves pushed the ship this way and that. As it collided with the rocks it made a terrible grinding sound. A jagged crack started to form along the ship's side.

The rainbow pony brushed against Grace's arm.

"We have to do something!" Grace told her. "I know the sailors shouldn't have used that net to catch you but I don't want anyone to get hurt." How she wished she had a magical stone so she

could speak to the pony properly!

The rainbow pony looked at Grace closely before diving away to join her friends. A moment later the sea ponies formed a circle and began moving in a graceful pattern. They cantered in and out of each other, keeping close but never touching. Twisting and turning, they almost seemed to stroke the sea with their beautiful flowing tails. The ocean around them started to shimmer as if magic was flowing into the water.

Grace swam hard to keep her head above the fierce waves. She watched every move of the sea ponies' dance. She knew the magical creatures wanted to help. She just hoped it wasn't too late.

With every nod of their heads and flick of their tails, the sea became quieter and the waves grew smaller. The ship lurched and bumped against the rocks a little more gently. With smooth, graceful movements, the sea ponies went on dancing.

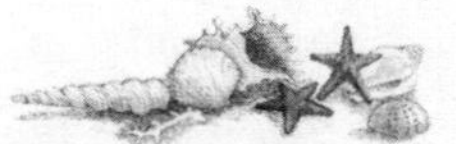

Chapter Seven
The Dance of the Sea Ponies

The twelve sea ponies galloped smoothly through the ocean. Sweeping their tails across the water, they stayed in a perfect ring. A shimmering light spread outwards from their circle and was gently washed away.

Grace watched, holding her breath. The crew of *The Royal Stickleback* stopped rushing around the deck to watch too. The waves grew softer, as if the ocean was rocked to sleep by the gentle pattern of the sea ponies' dance.

Grace swam back to the ship. She climbed

on board, helped by Maya and Sophy, and scrambled on to the deck just in time to hear Lady Cavendish telling off her crew. "What's the matter with you?" she snapped. "Stop staring at the animals and throw the net at them. They're all together so they'll be easy to catch!"

Some of the men shook their heads and others folded their arms. "No, My Lady," one of them said. "We can't do that. These magical creatures have calmed the sea and stopped this ship from smashing against the rocks. We can't hurt the ponies when they've saved our lives."

"Nonsense!" Lady Cavendish glared at them. "All that silly bobbing and splashing? I don't believe it helped at all."

The men still refused to have anything to do with catching the sea ponies. Lady Cavendish crossly threw the net herself, but it fell into the sea nowhere near the magical animals.

The sea ponies danced for a long time and Sophy and her friends watched them in delight. At last, heavy wing beats sounded in the air.

"Look, it's Windrunner!" said Sophy, waving happily at her dragon friend.

The huge storm dragon soared over the ship,

leading a flock of smaller sea dragons. Swooping down, he landed in the ocean with a gigantic splash. The little blue sea dragons flew down to the water beside him.

"Windrunner, you came to help us!" called Sophy.

The green dragon bowed his huge head and gave a long growl. Lady Cavendish gave a stifled shriek and tried to hide behind the mast of her ship.

"He's saying that Marella the sky unicorn was too far away to come back this time," Maya explained to Grace. "And he says that he and the sea dragons will carry everyone back to the safety of the beach."

The rainbow pony swam up to Windrunner and let out a stream of neighs and whinnies.

Sophy gasped.

"What is it?" asked Grace eagerly.

Sophy's blue eyes shone. "The sea ponies want to give you, me and Maya a ride all the way to

the Island of Ixus as a thank-you for helping them escape from the net. They say it's a special honour as no human has ever visited the island before!"

Grace's heart skipped a beat. "We get to ride on the sea ponies all the way to Ixus? That's the most awesome thing ever!"

"Thank you, we'd love to!" Maya called down to the ponies swimming in the turquoise water.

Grace waved at the sea ponies to show her thanks too. Secretly she wished she could have heard their invitation herself. If only she could understand them like the others!

"You'd better tell Lady Cavendish and the men what's happening," Maya said to Grace. "You're from Cala Sands and they'll probably listen to you."

"You're right!" Grace turned quickly to speak to the crew. "Listen, everyone! There's a big crack in the side of your ship so it's too dangerous to try to sail back to the harbour.

But don't worry! The dragons have offered to take you back to land. They'll carry you there safely."

One of the sea dragons took flight and hovered by the side of the ship. The men glanced worriedly from the girls to the dragon.

"Go on!" said Grace impatiently. "It's the only way you can get back to Cala Sands."

Hesitantly, one of the men climbed on to the dragon's back and the creature flew off in the direction of land. One by one, the sea dragons hovered beside the ship and the men clambered on to their backs. At last all the crew had flown away. The only grown-up left on board was Lady Cavendish and the only dragon in the sea was Windrunner.

"This is absolutely unthinkable!" Lady Cavendish folded her arms, her face as white as sea foam. "You *cannot* make me ride that monster. It's not normal! I refuse! Sir Fitzroy would never permit it!"

Windrunner rose into the air and hovered by the side of the ship so that she could climb on.

"There really isn't any other way back to land," said Maya.

"And Sir Fitzroy isn't here," added Sophy. "Not that he'd be able to do anything even if he was!"

"Help! There's a monster in the air!" cried Lady Cavendish, losing all composure.

"I don't think you should call the magical animal that's saving you a monster," said Grace. "It isn't very nice."

Lady Cavendish still refused to climb on to the dragon's back, so Windrunner swooped over the deck and seized her shoulders in his large claws. Then he lifted her from the ship and soared into the sky. Lady Cavendish squealed as they disappeared across the sea, her legs kicking in mid-air.

"Most people don't get a chance to fly," said Grace. "She really ought to be more grateful."

The sea ponies had been waiting patiently. Now they began whinnying to get the girls' attention.

"Are they saying it's time to go?" asked Grace.

"Yes, they can't wait to show us their island," said Maya.

"I can't wait to see it!" added Sophy. "After being awake all night I thought I'd feel tired but I'm just too excited!"

Grace dived into the calm blue sea. Bubbles streamed upwards as she swam to the surface.

"Jump in!" she called to the others. "Your dresses will get wet but they'll dry quickly in the sun later."

"OK, watch out!" Sophy jumped in, making a big splash.

Maya leapt in too. The girls came to the surface, laughing and splashing. The sea ponies swam round them, flicking water into the air with their noses.

Sophy laughed and flicked water back at them. Then she clapped as they swished their tails and leapt out of the water right in front of her.

Maya made friends with a small sea pony. He nuzzled her hand and she stroked his smooth coat. "That was brilliant – the way you danced to make the waves calm," she said. "I've loved watching you all."

Grace found the rainbow sea pony at her side. "Hello, friend!"

The pony whickered and swam round and

round her in excitement. Grace laughed. "Today has already been pretty amazing and I feel like the adventure's only just beginning!"

The pony gave a little jump and nudged Grace with her nose. Grace climbed on to her smooth white back, ready for the magical journey to the Island of Ixus.

Chapter Eight
The Island of Ixus

Grace rode across the water on the back of her rainbow sea pony. "Sophy! Maya! This is so much fun!"

Two sea ponies offered rides to the other girls. Sophy climbed on her pony's back eagerly.

Maya bit her lip. "How fast do you think they go? I don't want to fall off!"

"Just remember to hold on with your legs as well as your arms," said Grace. "Come on, Maya! You've flown on a sky unicorn. It's just the same!"

"It's not *exactly* the same!" said Maya, smiling a little.

The sea ponies neighed to each other as they galloped through the water.

At first, Grace concentrated on keeping her balance. The ocean breeze swept through her curly black hair. The broken ship disappeared behind them and for a while there was nothing but miles and miles of turquoise ocean speckled with little white waves. The sea ponies sped up and the ones leading the way made little leaps into the air.

Grace gazed at a patch of shimmering water

in the distance. It grew larger and larger until she realised it wasn't water at all – it was the Island of Ixus. She caught her breath. Ever since she was little, she'd heard tales about the island and the magical creatures that lived there. Now she *finally* had the chance to see it for herself!

The closer they got, the faster Grace's heart raced. She could see towering hills with sapphire waterfalls sweeping down them. A lush rainforest lay beyond the bright golden beach. The shimmering water around the island was filled with fish in every colour of the rainbow.

The sea ponies swam up to the shallows and the girls climbed off their backs. The water was warm and beautifully clear. Little baby turtles swam by the shore and seahorses darted among patches of blue and purple seaweed.

"Oops – sorry!" Sophy laughed, scooping up a baby turtle that had got caught in her skirt. She released him in the water next to his friends. "There you go!"

"They're adorable!" cried Maya as another turtle nibbled at her finger.

Grace stroked the rainbow pony.

"Thank you for the ride," she said softly. "I loved it!"

The pony nudged Grace with her nose, before swimming away to play with her friends. Grace sighed. She wished she could speak to the pony properly!

"Grace!" Sophy called from further up the beach. "We've found something to eat."

Grace ran to join the other girls. Together they pulled large orange fruit down from the trees. The fruit were deliciously sweet, especially when they were washed down with water from the sparkling waterfall.

After they'd had enough to eat, the girls played at jumping in and out of the waterfall. Then they went back to the sea to swim with the baby turtles and the sea ponies, and to dive for shells that lay on the sandy seabed.

Grace watched a starfish wriggle along the sand. "This island is amazing and we're the first people ever to see it!"

"I suppose once Windrunner and the sea dragons arrive we'll have to go back to the mainland," said Maya with a sigh. "I like it so much here. I don't want to go!"

"Me neither!" said Sophy. "But I have to go back to my maid duties at the castle and you have to go back to your travelling troupe. Anyway, we both need to be ready in case more magical animals need our help."

Grace dug her toe into the sand and frowned. "Do you think I could… I mean, would it be all right if I helped you to rescue magical creatures too?"

Sophy and Maya exchanged looks.

"We'd love you to help, but it would be quite tricky," said Sophy awkwardly. "You see, we get messages from the golden songbirds and sometimes Windrunner gives us important news. Not being able to talk to the magical animals would make it hard for you."

"We're really sorry," said Maya.

"But we'll fly over to visit you as often as we can!" added Sophy.

"It's OK!" Grace turned away so they couldn't see how sad she was. "I'm too busy fishing with my cousins to have time anyway."

"Look, the dragons are coming!" Sophy pointed at a cluster of dark specks in the sky. The specks grew larger with every second.

Windrunner and the sea dragons circled over the island. The sea dragons folded back their wings, plummeted through the air and landed, leaving huge claw marks in the sand. Windrunner plunged into the sea with a gigantic splash.

"Windrunner! You love landing in the water," laughed Sophy, running into the sea to hug him.

Windrunner growled a reply and swished water drops over his scaly back as if he wanted to cool down.

Grace noticed something purple floating on the surface of the water and realised it was

Sophy's little velvet bag – the one that held the magical stones. She dashed into the sea, but it sank before she could reach it.

"You dropped your bag, Sophy!" Grace waded to the place where it had sunk. The bag popped to the surface right in front of her, but when she picked it up it was empty.

Sophy took the bag. "Oh no! Where are all the stones?"

"Don't worry, I'll find them!" Grace dived under the turquoise water.

The stones were scattered across the sea bed. Their dark-grey colour made them easy to spot against the golden sand. Grace picked up a handful and returned to the surface to take a breath.

"Oh, thank you!" cried Sophy as Grace gave her the handful of wet stones.

"There are a few more. I'll fetch them for you." Grace dived down again, careful of the baby turtles swimming round her. She found three more stones and swam back to the surface.

"Well done, Grace!" Sophy beamed, adding the stones to the bag.

Grace plunged underwater for a third time. She couldn't see any more stones so she felt along the seabed with her fingers. "I can't find any more," she gasped as she bobbed up again.

"Oh dear!" Sophy's forehead creased. "I've counted them and I'm sure there's one missing."

Grace and Maya both dived under the water to search for the missing stone. Grace checked far and wide, looking under shells and pebbles. A little turtle swam up to her face before paddling into a cluster of swaying seaweed. The baby sea creature looked back at Grace with tiny black eyes.

It's almost as if he's trying to show me something, thought Grace. Gently, she pushed aside the fronds of seaweed and felt something rough hidden there.

She smiled as she picked up the little rock. She'd found the last one!

Her fingers tingled. The stone suddenly felt hot.

Surprised, Grace bobbed to the surface and stared at the little grey rock.

Maya came up for a breath too. "Are you all right?"

"Yes, it's the stone! It's … changing." Grace let the stone rest on the palm of her hand. An orange glow spread across its rough grey surface.

Sophy and Maya came closer and Windrunner bent his head to watch.

Just as Grace thought the rock was getting too hot to hold, it cracked open in her hand. The stone was hollow and the tiny cave inside was covered with beautiful deep-blue crystals.

"Wow!" breathed Grace. "Does that mean…?"

"Yes!" Sophy jumped up and down in the water, splashing them all. "It means you're one of us! This is your Speaking Stone and it truly belongs to you!"

Grace's cheeks went red. "I can't believe it! I didn't think the magic worked for me."

"Maybe you just needed to take your magical stone into the ocean," suggested Maya. "After all, you know all about the sea and your first rescue was an ocean creature."

"That's true!" Grace beamed a wide smile. "I've always loved sea ponies more than anything." She shaded her eyes, looking all around for her rainbow pony friend. She couldn't wait to talk to her!

Chapter Nine
The Map of Arramia

Holding her magical stone carefully, Grace swam out to where the sea ponies were playing.

"Hello! I've got something amazing to tell you!"

The sea ponies understood her at once and came leaping through the water to meet her.

"Sea girl!" said the rainbow pony. "You can speak to us!"

"I know! It's because of this magical stone that my friends gave to me." Grace showed them the stone. "My name is Grace and I've

wanted to talk to you all for so long!"

"Grace! What a lovely name," said the rainbow pony, and the others whinnied in agreement.

"What are you called?" Grace asked her.

"Coralli!" she neighed, and swished her tail.

Grace smiled at Coralli. "Thank you for bringing me here. I've always wanted to visit this

island. It's like a dream come true!"

Coralli bobbed her head. "We wished to thank you for stopping that horrible lady with the dangerous net."

"Lady Cavendish *is* horrible," agreed Grace. "But you still saved her and her crew."

"We believe in peace!" said Coralli. "We do not believe in harming other creatures."

Windrunner waded through the shallow water with Sophy and Maya riding on his back. "I have some good news about Lady Cavendish," he rumbled. "When I set her down on the beach at Cala Sands, she ran away as if there was a monster after her. I don't think she'll be bothering any magical animals again."

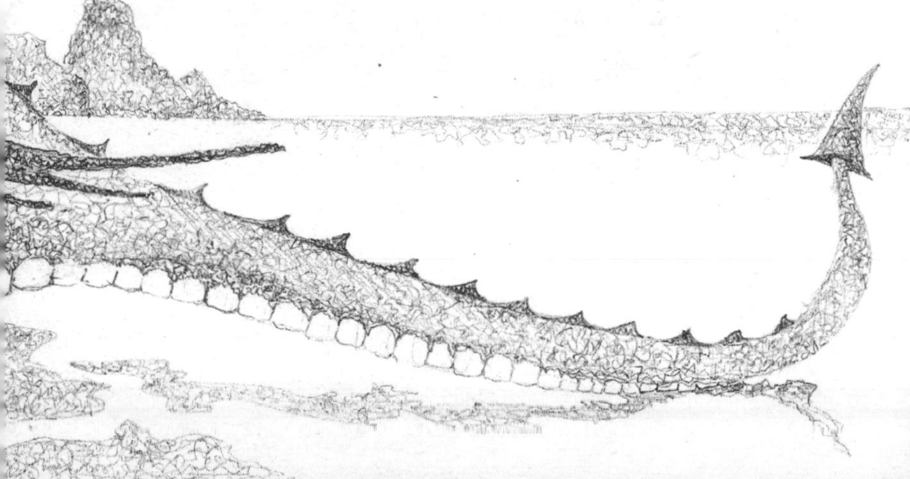

The girls clapped at this news and the sea ponies beat their hooves against the water.

As the sun began to set, Grace, Maya and Sophy said goodbye to the sea ponies.

Grace hugged Coralli. "I'll come to the beach to see you tomorrow. Maybe we can swim together again?"

"I'd love that!" replied Coralli. "I can show you all my favourite things: the pools where the pink anemones grow and the sea caves with the glittering rocks. There are so many places we can explore together!"

"That sounds brilliant!" Grace grinned. "I've had a wonderful time on the island. Thank you!"

Coralli whinnied and flicked water drops over Grace with her nose.

Windrunner, who'd been snoozing on the warm beach, woke up and stretched. "If you're ready, I'll fly you back home, Sophy. Would your

friends like a ride too?"

"Yes, please, Windrunner," said Maya. "I know Marella, my sky unicorn, can't fly over to meet me this time. She must be busy with the unicorn herd."

A sea dragon with a jagged blue crest on his back stopped beside them. "Excuse me, do you need a dragon ride of your own?" he asked Grace. "My name is Saltwing and it would be my honour to take you wherever you need to go. I will give you a ride any time you need one."

"That's a good idea!" cried Sophy. "That way, when we need your help you'll be able to fly over to find us, Grace."

"You're really kind," Grace told Saltwing. "Yes, please. I would like a ride."

Saltwing let her scramble on to his scaly back. "Are you ready, Grace the sea girl?"

Grace sat down and held tight to the crest sticking up from his back. "Yes, I'm ready!"

"Then let us fly!" Saltwing stretched his

deep-blue wings and took off.

Grace waved madly to Coralli as the dragon soared into the air. The breeze tickled her face and a funny swooping feeling in her stomach made her giggle. As they climbed higher, the ocean became a rumpled blue blanket dotted with tiny white waves. "This is awesome!" she called to Saltwing.

"Before we return to Cala Sands, let me show you our island from the air," said Saltwing. "We are so proud of our wonderful Island of Ixus." He zoomed downwards, flying low over the island so that she could see the jungle, the sparkling waterfalls and the rocky hills. Then, last of all, he glided over the sea. Baby turtles paddled in the shallows while sea ponies leapt through the deep waves.

"It's so beautiful," cried Grace. "I'll try to visit as often as I can!"

"We'd be very happy to see you," said Saltwing.

Windrunner glided over to join them, and Sophy and Maya waved from his back. "Do you like flying, Grace?" called Sophy. "Isn't it the best thing ever?"

"I love it!" called Grace.

At last they flew back over the calm ocean and landed on Cala Sands beach.

"Thank you, Saltwing," said Grace.

The blue sea dragon bowed. "It is my pleasure! Whenever you need me, tie a blue cloth to the window near the top of the lighthouse. I will see it and come to find you." He stretched his wings and flew away across the sea.

"I've been thinking," said Maya quietly. "Sir Fitzroy, the knight who hates magical creatures, sent letters all around the kingdom telling people to hunt the poor animals. So we should make sure that no more creatures are in immediate danger."

"That could take weeks!" exclaimed Sophy,

frowning. "Unless … maybe we could all check different places."

"Good idea!" said Grace. "I know Mr Wetherstone has a map of the whole kingdom. Let's ask him if we can look at it. Will you be all right here, Windrunner?"

"Of course!" The dragon lay down and dug his claws into the sand. "I shall have another snooze!"

The girls hurried past the swaying palm trees and climbed to the top of the cliff, where they knocked on the lighthouse door. Mr Wetherstone opened it and smiled when he saw them. "Back for another chocolate milkshake?"

"Well, actually we'd like to look at your map of the kingdom," Grace told him. "Would that be all right?"

"Of course! But you must have a milkshake too." The old man peered in the direction of the beach. "And maybe something nice for your dragon?"

Mr Wetherstone spread the large map out on his table and then began making drinks for everyone. Sophy took a bowlful of chocolaty drink down to the beach and Windrunner lapped it up with his big green tongue. It seemed that storm dragons liked chocolate milkshake very much!

Grace leaned over the old crinkled map. Apart from the fishing trips with her cousins, she'd never left Cala Sands. The sight of all the rivers and forests and mountains on the map made her insides turn a somersault.

"Why don't we each start with places close to where we live," said Maya sensibly. "My troupe travels across these lakes that are joined together by the River Arram, so I can check here." She pointed to three blue patches on the map. "Misty Lake, Gadfly Lake and Eagle Lake."

"I can search the forests and hills near the castle," said Sophy.

"I can check the cliffs and beaches all the way up to Dragon Point and Fire Rocks." Grace pointed to the rocks near the top of the map. "If I find any magical animals in trouble, I'll send you both a message." She smiled at her new friends. She couldn't wait to explore the Kingdom of Arramia. With her special new stone, she could help magical animals wherever she found them!

Have you read the first magical book in the series?

Paula Harrison

illustrated by SOPHY WILLIAMS

The Golden Songbird

Sophy hurried out of the castle door carrying a heavy wooden chair. She stopped at the bottom of the steps to get her breath back. Her arms ached from lifting things all morning!

A gentle breeze blew across the castle battlements, ruffling her wavy golden hair.

"Hurry up, Sophy! There's no time to dawdle." Mrs Ricker marched down the steps, her eyes bulging behind her spectacles. "And tie your hair back at once. I don't want the queen to see you looking so messy."

Mrs Ricker was the Royal Housekeeper. She was the kind of person who could spot untidy hair or a dirty apron from miles away!

"Yes, Mrs Ricker." Sophy searched her apron pocket for a hair bobble and quickly plaited her hair. Her parents had died when she was little and she'd worked as a maid at Greytowers Castle ever since. She was used to the housekeeper's strict ways.

Mrs Ricker went back inside. Sophy picked up the chair again and walked across the wooden drawbridge. The castle was circled by a moat filled with water and the drawbridge was the only way to get across.

When she reached the other side, Sophy set down the chair and gazed around. Greytowers Castle stood on a hill and the view from the top was amazing.

The Kingdom of Arramia stretched out in every direction, with its thick forests, bright rivers and majestic, snowy mountains.

Two planets hung together in the sky, a green one and a smaller purple one. Sophy loved the story of how the planets grew by magic in the air.

Enjoy more magical animal adventures at Zoe's Rescue Zoo!